TRADESMAN'S ENTRANCE

TRADESMAN'S ENTRANCE

© 2012 by Cameron Vale

ISBN: 978-0615644134

Vagabondage Press
PO Box 3563
Apollo Beach, Florida 33572
http://www.vagabondagepress.com

First print edition released in the United States of America and the United Kingdom, May 2012

10 9 8 7 6 5 4 3 2

Cover image by Vladimir Pomortse. Front cover design by Maggie Ward. Layout by N. Apythia Morges.

TRADESMAN'S ENTRANCE

Cameron Vale

Vagabondage Press

For E.W., S.N., and F.N., with love and thanks for your feedback and encouragement.

Act I
Unexpected: Stage Left

Clarissa tossed her auburn hair with a finely bejewelled hand and strode purposefully from the room. Bosom heaving with barely contained emotion, she grabbed her riding crop from the antique sideboard and slashed it viciously at a nearby potted palm, making it tremble as she headed for the garden. She was damned if she was going to let that cruel bastard Charles Hatherley see her cry ...

"Aw, wait a minute ... *shit!*"

With a weary sigh, Stephen bangs his forehead onto the computer keyboard with a resounding *thump* and grinds it there for a few seconds, sending a host of Hs, Js and Ys scattering across the screen like hungry insects.

"Fuck knows *why*, Clarissa, you silly tart. I mean, you've already let him see you cry copiously on pages 62, 86, 140 and 201. He's a complete *dickhead*, love. As far as I'm concerned, he's probably been having it off with your butler since page 1. You should have kneed him in the balls on page 2, and had done with it."

Straightening up, Stephen rests his key-thumped head wearily on one hand and starts to erase the erroneous letters messing up the page, then sighs once more and lets the *delete* button eat steadily back into the preceding offending paragraph. Unaware that talking to himself out loud has become a regular feature of his existence, he then announces to his chic but empty living room:

"Dear God, this is a complete pile of steaming *cack*. Why the hell did

I ever agree to do another Clarissa Hart novel? I'm so damn sick of the stupid, hormonal harpy and her pneumatically heaving breasts…"

Having witnessed this *particular* breakdown on a plenitude of occasions, the front door waves goodbye to patience and lets rip a series of short, staccato bangs, jumping the needle from the stuck record of Stephen's soliloquy.

Stephen, however, is lost in his own world.

"Aw, *great*, that's *all* I need. If that's another one of those dodgy bastards pretending to sell sodding tea towels for charity again, they're gonna get what for."

Jumping away from the computer, Stephen marches automatically to the hallway, words of dismissal already flying from his lips before the front door is fully open.

"Sorry, I'm *busy*. I don't want *anything*."

"Don'tcha? You're a one-off then, ain'tcha? Everyone wants *something*, mate."

Staring puzzled into empty space, Stephen finally follows the siren-call chuckle warming the air to his left. With surprise, he registers a grinning vision wreathed in casual smoke, leaning against the porch wall as if "Nonchalance" was a middle name.

Stephen gulps.

Loudly.

Instead of the expected spotty, ASBO-d reject, a tall, tanned Adonis stands before him, sprung straight from the pages of one of his over-wrought novels — dark, shoulder-skimming hair glinting copper in the sunlight, tastily trim and muscular body squeezed, but not entirely contained, by a low-slung pair of blue jeans and a tight, white workman's vest.

In the beat of silence that follows, Stephen reminds his eyelids how to blink and his mouth to speak.

"Pardon?"

The Tanned Adonis merely flicks his spent rolled-up cigarette in the general direction of Stephen's front garden and grins a little wider.

"I said, everyone wants *something*, mate. Cats want milk. Dogs want a bone. Capitalism wants a good kicking, and you want the plumber you called out an hour ago. Am I right?"

Inwardly adding breathing to his reminder list of things to do, as cochlea informs brain of an uncommonly sexy-slurred voice, Stephen checks his watch.

"*Two* hours, 47 minutes ago, *actually*. I've been waiting so long, I'd completely forgotten I'd called you out."

This sarcastic information merely receives a sanguine shrug.

"Mate. What can I tell you? This is London, innit? You gotta account for the traffic. I was sat on my numbed arse going precisely nowhere for over a bleedin' *hour* on the Shepherd's Bush roundabout earlier. Thought I was gonna have to start writing my last will and testament. Still, you don't want to hear about my troubles, do yer? Show us yer pipes and I'll get cracking."

As The Tanned Adonis sweeps his tool bag from the porch floor and steps forward, Stephen shoots out a warning hand to hold him back.

"Wait. Hang on a minute. Can I see your ID card?"

"My *what?*"

"Your ID card. You could be anyone."

The Tanned Adonis regards Stephen quizzically for a moment, grey-green eyes a-glint and twinkled by the late-day sun.

Not to mention wry amusement.

"Well, I *could* be anyone, but I'm fuckin' *not*. Name's Dave. And I'm arsed if I can remember what the hell I've done with my ID card, if I ever had one to start with. So, do you want those pipes fixed or don't you? You're my last job of the day, and I'm more than happy to piss off down the pub early, if you don't. S'lovely day for basking topless in the beer garden, 's far as I'm concerned. Choice is yours, mate."

Stephen weighs up the frightening prospect of inviting a stranger into his home who could be a burglar or murderer or *both* against the much more appealing prospect of watching that tantalising tanned, toned body at work for the next hour of his life. Realising the latter option might be a very welcome distraction from wrestling with Clarissa's heaving bosom, he opens the door for Dave to enter. However, as the Adonis of Plumbing is about to cross the threshold, Stephen knee-jerks again to block the doorway, jabbing an accusatory finger at Dave's muddy work boots.

"Sorry, could you wipe your feet before you come in?"

Dave glances down at his offending footwear then shoots Stephen a cheery smile, his voice airy.

"Ok, squire. Not a problem. Can do. OCD, are we?"

"No, of course not. I've just got white carpets, they're new, and…"
Stephen stops, realising that he doesn't have to explain his recent interior
decorating fit of pique to a tardy plumber, no matter how attractive. "Just
wipe your feet, ok? Kitchen's this way."

Dave follows Stephen into the hallway and through to the source of
the problem. A swift stomp across pristine carpets, past lavender walls
hung with Mapplethorpe photography results in an achingly trendy
space-age, metallic-surfaced kitchen equipped with everything from
dainty cappuccino cups to a puzzlingly prominent pasta press. Dave
unceremoniously dumps his battered tool bag on the kitchen table with
a resounding clunk.

"Nice pad. Shame you don't have many people round."

Stephen turns back, frowning at the confounding accuracy of this
statement from the mouth of a complete stranger.

"What on *earth* made you say that?"

Dave winks cheekily.

"White carpets, mate. Not one for parties, are ya?"

Irritation rapidly replacing attraction due to the cockiness lurking in
Dave's smile, Stephen huffs, "Look, just fix the bloody blockage, would
you? I'm really busy. I've got … *stuff* to do next door, so I'll just leave you
to it, shall I?"

However, as he storms back toward the lounge, a suddenly plaintive
voice calls from the kitchen, all arrogance gone.

"Aw, *mate*. Pop the kettle on first, eh? I'm as parched as the Gobi.
Haven't stopped for a minute since breakfast. My stomach thinks my
throat's been cut."

Turning back, Stephen regards him for a moment, eyes drifting to
the lithe, muscled arm propped casually against his kitchen doorway,
revealing a masculine nest of glossy, black hair in a finely arched armpit.
Feeling his irritation begin to drown under an inner tidal wave of
mounting lust, Stephen speedily surfs his gaze back to the relative safety
of Dave's pleading face.

"Ah, go *on*, mate. One teabag, three sugars. That's *all* I'm asking."

* * *

Waiting for the kettle to boil, Stephen struggles to avert his gaze from Dave's elevated rear poking out from under his sink, low-slung jeans slipping steadily southward. Every move reveals a curved expanse of tightly packed Calvin Klein's. Each hitch of the vest slipping upward exposes sunken back dimples that Stephen can't help but imagine licking endlessly in some parallel universe.

Eventually, Dave's airily cheerful voice comes drifting out from beneath the sink, dragging Stephen back into the present-leaden world with a resounding inner *thump.*

"So, who d'ya reckon for the footie this year, then?"

Realising with shame that his tongue is quite literally hanging out, Stephen snaps his mouth shut, wincing as tender skin catches sharp-edged molar, before dragging his pained attention back to the whistling kettle. Producing teacups from the shelf above him, honesty chasing sensual hunger from his lips, Stephen mutters "Can't *abide* football."

In response, Dave's cupboard-clamped, yet cheerful voice drifts back through the sinkhole.

"More of a ballet man, eh?"

Stirring the teabags around in the pot much harder than necessary in irritation, Stephen slops a little tea onto the spotless work surface and automatically reaches for a cloth to mop up the mess, his shoulders tensing defensively.

"And what is *that* supposed to mean?"

"Oh, nothing. Just shooting the breeze, my friend. If yer not into one, chances are yer into the other, if you know what I mean. Personally, I can take a bit of both."

A cacophony of clanging metal-against-metal erupts from under the sink, making Stephen jump as he pours the tea from the pot. Automatically, he reaches again for the cloth to contain the spillage. Meanwhile, from down below, Dave merrily resumes his firearm attack on the breeze.

"Shagged a dancer once when I was tweaking the lead pipes at one of them fancy West End theatres. You wouldn't *believe* the positions those hoofers can wind themselves into. Turned into quite a rum do in the end, as a matter of fact."

Stephen carefully drops three heaped spoonfuls of sugar into one of the cups and snorts at the comedic image of athletic sex performed in dingy dressing rooms that stink of greasepaint and slopped gin before returning his longing gaze to Dave's mesmerisingly pert behind.

"No, I'm quite sure I wouldn't believe you, so please spare me the details."

"God, these pipes of yours are in a right state. What the bleedin' hell've you been chucking down here, eh? Glue? Hang on, I'll have to fetch me big tools. Bloody waste pipe connector's bunged up something chronic."

As Dave unexpectedly emerges from beneath the sink with a cheery, "Ooh, ta. Got any biscuits, then?" Stephen realizes with horror that he's been caught in the act of voyeurism. Guiltily handing Dave his cup, Stephen spins away to the fridge to fetch some milk and hide his blush, sarcasm leaping to his lips to cover his discomfort.

"Yes, I've got biscuits. I've also got cake. But the biggest thing I've got at the moment is a blocked pipe that's staying blocked while you lounge around my kitchen taking afternoon tea."

In the silence that follows his outburst, Stephen feels the cold shiver of scrutiny on his back and knows that Dave is watching him, in all likelihood leaning casually against the worktop, sipping his warm brew. Stephen barks himself a strict internal order to turn around and check reality, but finds that his stubborn feet aren't built for listening. While he berates himself for cowardice, an easy voice cuts through the inner static.

"Can't have a cuppa without biscuits, mate. That's treason, that is. Poor bastards have ended up in Guantanamo Bay for less."

Stephen glares back at Dave for a second in puzzlement, then, finding the curved, compact muscles on Dave's crooked arm so arresting he can feel himself harden, he swiftly returns his attention to locating the lactose, focusing his mind on Dave's words, rather than his body, for safety.

"I'm sorry. You've really lost me, now. I totally fail to see what biscuits have to do with politics. Nor do I think it will improve my quality of life to find out."

Dave, however, seems blithely oblivious to a level of sarcasm that could strip the marble from the worktops. Instead of backing down, he takes another enthusiastically noisome hit of tea, and apparently decides to expand.

"Little theory of mine. It's like this: Yer working classes are yer plain digestive wholemeal biscuits. Simple, honest, always getting dunked in the hot stuff. Yer middle classes are yer fake chocolate Bourbons. Pretending to be fancy, but not really. Taste like shit. And yer upper classes are yer chunky Kit Kat fat cats. Cold as hell 'cos they can afford to live in fancy fridges. Break yer teeth as soon as look at yer. Follow me?"

Feeling his embarrassing erection mercifully fade again in response to the complete nonsense his ears have just been subjected to, Stephen turns around with a sigh.

"Not in the slightest. What in God's name are you on about?"

Dave takes a further noisy slurp of tea and smacks his lips appreciatively.

"Think about it. The trouble with this country is, no one's happy to be a humble Digestive anymore. They're all fake Bourbons pretending to be fat cat Kit Kats. I always think you can tell a lot about a man by the biscuits he keeps in his cupboard."

Dave nods at the storage units behind Stephen's head.

"What y'hiding in there, then?"

"Fondant Fancies."

"I'll go get me other tool bag."

* * *

Once Dave has ventured back to his van, Stephen relocates to the living room where Clarissa and her heaving bosom are waiting.

"Right, c'mon Clarry, love. Sorry I called you a tart earlier. Meant nothing by it. This writer's block's just getting me down. Let's see if we can nail this chapter before God's Gift to Plumbing and Politics finishes his tea."

Setting his cup down at the side of the computer screen, Stephen starts to type, gripped by sudden inspiration, fast fingers flying over the keyboard with renewed resolve.

Clarissa tossed her auburn hair with her finely bejewelled hand then flashed Charles a brutally triumphant smile, strong white teeth glinting in the sunlight.

"I don't give a damn if you've been seeing someone else, Charles. In fact, I'm glad. D'you hear me? Glad. The truth is, I've been having it off with my

plumber for the last six months and he's twice the man you'll ever be."

Bosom heaving with barely contained emotion, Clarissa grabbed her riding crop from the antique sideboard and slashed it viciously across Charles Hatherley's startled face.

"You're a rotter and a cad. And don't think for one minute I'm unaware that you've been rogering my butler rigid when my back is turned. Poor Bartlett's been carrying a limp for weeks. It's over, Charles ...."

"Hello? You still there, mate? I'll just carry on, shall I?"

Stephen jumps at the sound of Dave's voice calling from the kitchen, then frowns at the irritating interruption.

"I think that's the general idea, isn't it? When you've finished your tea, of course. Don't let my plumbing emergency interrupt your refreshments."

"Cheers. Mind if I help myself to a Fondant Fancy, then?"

With a heavy sigh, Stephen springs from his seat and prowls back to the kitchen where Dave is casually lounging against the still-blocked sink, prising the lid off a treasured family cake tin with filthy fingers. Meanwhile, a raised-tempo'd tattoo to the temples keeps Stephen informed of his blood pressure status.

"Look, is there any chance of fixing my blockage before you eat me out of house and home? Or should I nip down the supermarket and get in more supplies?"

Amused marine eyes shoot up to challenge Stephen's Death Star glare.

"Alright, mate. Keep yer hair on. That's a lovely barnet you've got on you, there. Must've taken you hours to get it looking like that. Be a shame to lose it."

Dave tosses the cake tin lid aside with a clattering flourish swiftly followed by a smirk.

"Just one quick Fancy, then I'll get me ratchet out. How's that? There's an offer you can't refuse."

Confused by Dave's possible innuendo and unsure about his motives, Stephen watches him rummage in the cake tin for a further moment, then mutters tightly, "Just don't eat the pink ones, ok? They're my favourites."

Dave stares at Stephen for a second, the twinkle in his countenance increasing, then he pulls a yellow Fondant Fancy from the tin and pops it in his mouth in one. Grabbing his ratchet from the kitchen table, he drops to his knees and crawls back under the sink, elevated rear once more drawing Stephen, step-by-creeping-step, magnetically back into the kitchen, mind focused on a work of art in progress…

Until Dave's triumphant voice stops him in his tracks.

"Bloody *knew* it. Had you pegged as a wrong 'un, the moment I clapped eyes on you."

Stephen's fists clench tight in anger, a flash-flush of outrage burning neck and face, the tattooed pulse-in-head increasing, *tarantella*.

"How fucking *dare* you! What gives you the right to come into my home nearly three hours bloody late with muddy work boots, drink my tea and eat my cake and *then* insult me to my face?"

From under the sink, Dave glances back over his shoulder, eyes widened with surprise.

"Who says I meant it as an insult? I'm a wrong 'un, too, when the mood takes me. Equal opportunities for all, I say. That's democracy in action for you."

Tossed off balance by Dave's unexpected response, Stephen stumbles to a kitchen chair and sits down shakily, his voice still tight with anger.

"You talk an awful lot of *crap* for a plumber, you know that? That's not democracy in action. I'll tell you what democracy in action is, *my friend*. Democracy in action is getting the shit kicked out of you from one end of the school playground to the other for 12 sodding years of your life. It's getting called a poof and a ponce and a *wrong'un* by every Tom, Dick or Harry who ever came within 10 friggin' yards of you. It's wanking off to daytime telly every sodding day because you're too fucking scared to leave the house in case you get *gay-bashed.*"

Dave immediately stops fiddling with the sink pipe and re-emerges into the light, face stunned.

"Fuckin' hell! *Every* day? To *daytime* telly?"

Blushing furiously, Stephen turns away, wishing he could claw the treacherous words back from the ether or delete them with a keyboard stab.

"I was speaking rhetorically. 'Course I don't do that."

Dave sits back on his heels and regards Stephen's turned, flushed cheek for a moment, twirling his spanner around in his fingers like a majorette baton, biting his lower lip in an apparent effort to contain a smile.

"Bet you bloody well do. Many a true word spoken in anger, as they say. Now I see why you went for the white carpets."

Leaping from his chair, Stephen stalks back to the safety of the living room, his retreating retort yelled loud enough to make the Mapplethorpes rattle on the wall.

"Fucksake. Look. I've had enough of this bollocks. Just fix my sodding pipe and fuck *off*, will you?"

As Stephen once more settles himself down at the computer and attempts to wrestle his heartbeat under control, Dave's amiable voice comes drifting down the hallway.

"Well, since you asked so nicely....Smashing cuppa, by the way. 'S'done me a world of good. Calm down, alright? I'm on it."

* * *

Clarissa tossed her auburn hair with her finely bejewelled hand then flashed Charles a brutal snarl, her strong, white teeth flashing feral in the sunlight.

"I don't give a flying fuck if you've been seeing someone else, Charles, you bastard. In fact, I'm bloody thrilled. D'you hear me? Thrilled. The truth is I've been shagging my plumber from pillar to post for the last six months and he's 10 times the man you'll ever be."

Bosom shuddering with violent emotion, Clarissa grabbed her riding crop from the antique sideboard and slashed it viciously across Charles Hatherley's overfed behind, making him jump in shock.

"Take that, you swine! You're a rotter and a cad. And don't think for one minute I don't know you've been buggering my butler backwards into tomorrow when you thought I wasn't looking, you pathetic, little runt. It's over, Charles, for good this time."

"Gotcha, y'*bastard!* Hey, mate? I'm getting somewhere now. Have this fixed in a jiffy. What's yer name then, eh?"

Stephen slams a palm to the computer keyboard in frustration, sending Clarissa and Charles once more fleeing up the page hotly pursued by errant letters, then he spins a similar path back to the kitchen.

"Oh, for fuck*sake*. It's Stephen. Why?"

Dave sticks his head out from under the sink, his voice ratcheting down a notch from cheerful to placatory.

"Look, Steve, I didn't mean anything by what I said earlier. It was just a turn of phrase, y'know? Like I said, I'm a bit partial myself on occasion. Honest."

Rolling his eyes in disbelief, Stephen throws himself back into the seat by the kitchen table.

"A bit *partial*? You make it sound so bloody *simple*, don't you? Like deciding whether to have a Digestive or a frigging Kit Kat to dunk in your tea."

"Well, it is, isn't it?"

Stephen sighs and drops his gaze to hands held suddenly useless in his lap, then shakes his head despairingly.

"No. No, it bloody well *isn't*."

Putting his ratchet aside, Dave shuffles out from under the sink, his tone softening.

"Y'been having a bit of trouble hooking up with the fellas, then?"

"Jesus ..."

Stephen stares at his fidgeting fingers for a moment more in silence, the desire to open up to someone, *anyone,* waging war with his embarrassment. Eventually, he shoots Dave a vulnerable look, his voice barely a whisper.

"You could say that, yes."

Holding Stephen's gaze for a moment, Dave gives a sympathetic smile then arches an eyebrow.

"Well, if you stopped wanking off to daytime telly and actually *left the house occasionally*, you'd up yer chances. Sorry to point that out to you but, it's bleedin' obvious, innit?"

Anger mounting all too easily on the back of shame, Stephen glares at Dave, unaware that his twisting hands are retracting to fists in his lap.

"I don't wank off to daytime telly, ok? Let's just get that *crystal clear.* "

Dave replies lightly, "'Torchwood,' then?"

"*Bastard.*"

With a grin, Dave picks up his ratchet again and resumes work.

"Aw, mate. It was just a guess. Didn't think I'd hit the nail on the head first time. Calm down, ok? Nothing wrong with the old five finger shuffle, is there? Although, you might wanna try going for a later telly timeslot — or better still, a different gogglebox altogether. There's much better stuff online for that kinda shenanigans, if you ask me. Been known to have the odd hand shandy at the keyboard m'self when the mood strikes. Bottom line is, it's a sad old world we live in. You've got to take yer pleasures where you can."

Stephen watches Dave's own bottom line shimmying from side to side in time to his arm movements for a moment, then mutters, "I thought I'd phoned a plumber not a philosopher. There must be a couple of pages stuck together in my Yellow Pages."

Dave glances over his shoulder at Stephen, eyebrow once again raised.

"Yeah, well, we all know *why*, don't we?"

"Oh, *piss off.*"

After an extended spell of resumed metallic cacophony, Dave chuckles and emerges from under the sink again with a friendly smile and an outstretched hand.

"And I thought you were a nice, polite but uptight Kit Kat when you opened the door. All the swear words are coming out now. You're a right little Digestive on the quiet, aren'tcha? Anger suits ya, mind. Brings a bit of colour to yer cheeks. Now. Hand me those pliers."

Stephen follows Dave's pointing finger to the tabletop toolbox, then coolly returns Dave's gaze, folding his arms tightly across his chest.

"Please?"

Dave drops his voice back to a soothing croon and mockingly bats his eyelashes.

"*Pretty* please."

Sulkily repressing a smile, Stephen relents and plonks the requested item into Dave's outstretched hand.

"Here you go, sodding Socrates."

As Dave crawls back under the sink and leans forward with both hands, struggling to unscrew the pipe fitting with the pliers, Stephen watches the dance of his behind, jeans riding a little lower, pulling the Calvin Kleins with them to reveal a hint of puzzlingly *tanned* butt-cleavage. Having allowed himself a quick brain-skirmish through the possibilities of home tanning beds, nudist colony membership and double-jointed beauty product application, Stephen then crash lands his distracted cerebellum on the shores of a much more important question.

"So… how *do* you hook up with the *fellas* when the mood takes you and you're feeling a bit *partial*, then, seeing as you're apparently such a shag monster?"

Dave gives the pipe connection a firm tug, making it squeak as the copper fitting grinds against years of scale build-up on the pipe, then he tosses the pliers aside and starts to twist the connector by hand.

"Great footballer, Socrates. Played for Brazil. Ok, let's see.… Well, you just catch their eye, don'tcha? In a bar or a club or whatever. Clock 'em giving yer the old sideways glance when they think yer not looking. Sidle over. Sound them out. Bit of safe footie or music chat to kick things off. Keep it neutral and blokey to start with, then drop in the odd innuendo, see if they take the bait. If they don't and start to get angsty, pull the innocent card, call *them* a queer first and walk off in high dudgeon. If they do rise to the bait, go in for the kill. Bob's yer Aunty Mary. Simple."

Stephen shakes his head in disbelief and sighs heavily.

"Jesus…simple for *you*, maybe…"

With a final wrench, Dave frees the pipe from its recalcitrant fitting and swiftly pulls a bucket under the freed pipe to catch the blocked residue. As the pipe continues to drain into the bucket, he turns back to Stephen with a smile.

"And just *occasionally*, you come to fix their pipes, get chatting and miss the night bus home, as it were."

Thunderstruck, Stephen stares at Dave's smiling face for a second, unable to believe the evidence of his own ears. Finally, the foreplayed mental jigsaw clicks firmly into place.

"Would you like another cup of tea?"

"Y'gonna throw another Fondant Fancy in with that?"

"You can even have a pink one, if you like."

"You're on."

* * *

One hour, three cups of tea and an empty cake tin later, Dave finally emerges from under the sink, hoists up his wandering jeans and strolls over to the kitchen table.

"There, all done. Good as new. You're sorted."

Gathering up the cups and depositing them in the sink, Stephen mutters sarcastically over his shoulder, "Just as well. I'm down to my last teabag."

Without missing a beat, Dave fishes a tin of cleanser out of his tool bag and starts to coat his blackened hands as he saunters back to the sink, nudging Stephen out of the way so he can rinse them under the running water.

"Better crack open a beer then, eh? It's gone six, and you and me are still sober. That's a disaster that wants fixing."

Shivering at the ice-warm contact of Dave's bare arm on his own, Stephen takes a faltering step back and murmurs automatically.

"I don't drink beer, sorry. Makes me put on weight. I'm on The Montignac."

Dave frowns at Stephen over his shoulder.

"The Monty-*what?*"

"The Montignac diet. It's a GI diet."

"Sorry, mate. You've lost me. What's the Second World War got to do with losing weight? D'you stuff yerself with powdered egg or what?"

Stephen giggles, feeling his whole body relax in response to Dave's confusion.

"Not that kind of GI, silly. GI stands for glycaemic index."

Dave finishes rinsing his hands and starts to look around for a towel.

"I hope yer gonna finish that last sentence in English for me."

Fetching a cloth from the Kubrick-inspired, monolith rack, Stephen hands it to him.

"Glycaemic index is a measure of blood sugar. Some foods make you put on weight because they raise your blood sugar too high, too fast. Montignac was the Frenchman who first based a diet around it. Top of the no-no list is beer. That's why men end up with beer bellies."

Dave tosses the used towel playfully back to Stephen and leans against the worktop, one newly clean hand shoving his vest upward to reveal a fully-toned six-pack.

"Sorry, mate. I drink it every day and there's nothing wrong with this belly."

Stephen stares for a moment at the movement of Dave's fingers as he pats his perfectly flat stomach, then whispers,

"Well, you've got a point there…"

Then, registering that Dave is watching him with a coolly amused grin, Stephen feels a flicker of irritation at his companion's smugness and lashes out without thinking.

"But that's because you're still young, isn't it? Your metabolism's sky-high. Give it 10 years of aging and boozing, and you'll look like every other fat bastard waddling up the high street, in need of lunchtime lipo and a man-bra."

Dave's smug grin immediately disappears under a veil of thinly disguised hurt.

"Well, thanks very much. That's put a right old black cloud on my sunny horizon."

Guiltily, Stephen ventures a placatory smile.

"I've got some red wine. That's allowed in moderation. Want some?"

Dave stares back at Stephen's pleading eyes for a second, then shrugs and returns the smile.

"Never touched the stuff. Always had it down as a bird's drink. But, since I'm well on the way to being Gary Gutbucket, according to you and yer friend Monty, guess now's the time to try it, eh?"

With relief, Stephen reaches into the cupboard behind him for the wine.

"It's a really good Chianti Classico."

"I'm sure it is, love. Well done, you."

* * *

While Stephen fetches wine glasses and sets them on the table, then uncorks the wine, on the other side of the kitchen, Dave watches silently, noting the tremor in his employer's shaking fingers. Finally, he smirks, "Bet those Fondant Fancies aren't part of old Monty's diet sheet."

Stephen hands Dave his glass of red wine, a similar blush of colour forming on his cheek.

"No, 'course they're not. Trouble with dieting is, every now and then you crack and stuff your face with cake. Or I do, anyway."

Dave takes a long, grateful slug of the alcohol, immediately noting its smoothness and strength in comparison to beer and makes a mental note to partake of a smaller amount next time. As he pulls the half-empty glass down from his lips, the sight of Stephen watching him wide-eyed and open-mouthed fills his vision, making him grin.

Eventually, Stephen murmurs, "Like it?"

Feeling his entire body relax as the alcohol hits his stomach, Dave watches Stephen take a daintily small sip of his own drink, the residue of the wine passing over his lips leaving a hint of colour behind, then he instinctively steps forward, closing the distance between them.

"Yeah, s'alright. Slips down easy enough. Like all good things in life."

Sensing the air crystallising around them as Stephen freezes in shock, Dave grins and rubs a teasing thumb against Stephen's mouth.

"Stains yer lovely lips red 'n' all."

The sharp intaken breath against his thumb feels like an "all systems go" signal to Dave. Leaning forward, he presses his lips against Stephen's own, but soon withdraws, puzzled at the lack of initial response. Then, feeling Stephen breathe out again sharply as he stumbles against him, Dave grins and winds his fingers into the back of Stephen's hair, pulling him closer for a deeper kiss, enjoying the subtle tremor of uncharted body under pressing fingertip as he trails both hands firmly down Stephen's back.

Fucking knew you wanted this as much as I did.

* * *

Meanwhile, on the other end of the kiss, Stephen is wondering, *Who is at the front door this time?* Then it hits him that the hammering sound in earshot is his own heart making a break for freedom against his trembling ribcage. Stephen gasps for air as Dave eventually releases him with a smile and a smudged thumb once more at his mouth, Dave's murmured words emerging wine-warmed and lust-lazy.

"Soft old lips you've got on you there. Like a girl's. Very nice."

As Stephen tries not to sway in shock, Dave casually wanders back to his former position lounging by the worktop.

"So, what was this 'stuff' I was holding you back from doing in the other room then? Was 'Torchwood' on?"

Gripping the kitchen table for support, Stephen stares, sightless, into his wineglass, mind still reeling at what just happened, and murmurs on autopilot.

"No. Look, stop going on about that, will you? It's embarrassing."

Dave takes another smaller sip of wine and shrugs.

"Nothing to be embarrassed about, mate. It's just a natural impulse. If The Man Upstairs hadn't intended us to play games, he wouldn't have given us a joystick. Go on, then. Show us how you do it. I'm always up for learning new techniques."

Snapping out of his fugue, Stephen's shocked eyes flash upward to meet Dave's twinkling gaze, his wine and kiss-blushed mouth opening in horror.

"If you think for one *minute* I'm going to stand in my own kitchen and show you how I *wank* an hour after meeting you, you must be insane. I don't even *know* you."

Dave shoots out a placatory hand.

"Alright, *alright*. Calm down. Keep yer hair on. Was just a suggestion, mate. You were well up for a snog, so I thought I'd move things on a bit. Looks like I misjudged a little. I'm sorry, ok?"

Dave shrugs and takes another sip of wine.

"See, thing is ... while you were having the shit kicked out of you from one end of the playground to the other, I was in the playground *toilets* with a cute kid called Trevor. Quite the exhibitionist, was old Trev. Learnt a lot from watching him. He got shoved in the slammer years later for getting his todger out on the tube at Mile End. Nearly gave some poor old Doris a heart attack, so she reported him to the filth."

Dave drains the dregs of his wine and returns the glass to the worktop, twirling the thin stem around between finger and thumb, seemingly lost in memory, a mischievous smile dancing at the corners of his mouth.

"He used to send me some right racy letters from the clink. Getting banged up turned out to be a bit of a blessing in disguise for old Trev. Fuck knows, it certainly kept me well entertained. But that's another story ..."

Waving his empty wineglass at Stephen, Dave's grin widens.

"Got any more of that Canty-Whotsit? I'm getting partial to it. Slips down a treat, doesn't it?"

Stephen's hand lingers uncertainly on the bottle.

"You're driving though, aren't you?"

Dave takes a step forward and plonks his glass down on the table, his voice quiet but firm.

"Yeah. But not necessarily *tonight*, eh?"

As soon as the ringing in Stephen's ears has ceased and he's sure he's not *actually* going to faint, he focuses on controlling his shaking hand as he refills Dave's glass, then wonders why he suddenly feels his earlier anger returning. Eventually, he realises that it's Dave's quiet confidence that's the trigger.

"So, this is your technique then, is it? Is this how you chat guys up? *Show us how you wank.* Straight out with it. Just like *that.*"

Dave takes his refilled glass back to the worktop and shrugs, bemused.

"S'pose so. Never really thought about it, to be honest. I'm just being myself, you know? Just being straight. You should pardon the pun."

Stephen takes a bigger gulp of his own wine than intended and tries to suppress a cough, shaking his head in disbelief.

"It's not a p— Look. Don't you ever get beaten up? I mean you're pretty bloody *forward*. Hasn't some bloke ever turned around and decked you when you talk to them like that?"

Dave considers this for a moment as he takes another sip of his drink. Cool green eyes focusing above the glass rim on Stephen's flushed, pained face.

"Well, first off, I don't go out *expecting* to get beaten up, like you do. I don't have 'hit me' plastered all over my boat race. First thing marines do when they're off on a secret mission is they whack on some camouflage, right? And secondly, I'm only this forward with blokes who look like they'd be up for it. Basic law of the jungle, innit? Gotta keep yer wits about you at all times."

Stephen can't help chuckling at Dave's oddly military approach to gay dating.

"God, you're a right bleedin' Rambo, you are."

Then the wine starts to hit home, a hot flash of relaxation burning off the embers of his anger, making him feel giggly as another thought strikes him. "You're Rambo and I wish I was *Rimbaud*."

Dave grins before shaking his head.

"Sorry, mate. There's nothing remotely Rambo about you. No offence. That's yer problem."

"No, I meant ... doesn't matter. Look, shall we sit down or something?"

Dave saunters back to the table and picks up the wine bottle. And for a panicky moment, it flits through Stephen's reeling mind that his life-long, innate indecisiveness is about to be flattened by military-precision insurgence. Dave doesn't disappoint.

"I've got a better idea. I'll grab what's left of this bottle, you grab the other bottle I clocked in the back of that cupboard, then you show me where you keep yer bedroom."

Unexpectedly, Stephen freezes, his whole body gaining a couple of inches in height as former tension returns. Eyes widening in fright, he ducks his head so suddenly, Dave takes a step backward in apparent puzzlement.

"What?"

Stephen's mumbled reply is addressed to Dave's feet.

"Nothing ... it's just ..."

With a frown, Dave returns the wine bottle to the table along with his glass.

"Have I got me wires crossed, here? I thought you were up for it."

Stephen's eyes dart up to plead with Dave's then duck down again.

"I am ... it's just ..."

Smiling again at the spoken affirmation, Dave steps closer, rubs a teasing palm against Stephen's jeans and murmurs softly, "Well, yer hard enough, alright. Hope this is feeling as good to you as it does to me."

The hammering on the front door that Stephen heard earlier is now resounding off every wall, every window and every work surface. Panicking, he grips Dave's wrist in desperation to stop his movements, arousal weakening his legs, alarm tightening his chest.

"Fuck. Look. I haven't done this before, ok?"

Chuckling, Dave tips Stephen's chin up with a finger so he can see his eyes.

"What? Had sex with a bloke? Pull the other one. You're gay as a bag full of bunting, you are."

In response, Stephen's own fingers latch onto a corner of Dave's vest and tug childlike, unthinkingly.

"No. I meant had sex with *anyone*."

This time it's Dave's turn to freeze, mouth dropping open in disbelief.

"You're fuckin' *kidding* me? What age are you?"

Stephen shuts his eyes in shame and groans, "Twenty-sodding-six."

Eyes narrowing in suspicion, Dave takes a step backward, pulling his vest out of Stephen's grip.

"What are you? Some kinda Christian nutter?"

"No."

"Yer not one of them kiddie-fiddlers, are yer?"

"*God*, no!"

"What is it then? Don't tell me you like getting frisky with Fido."

Stephen spins away from Dave in frustration, his raised voice echoing off the cold metallic surfaces of the kitchen.

"Fucksake, *no!* I fancy blokes, *alright?* And the odd girl, as long as she looks like a bloke. ... It's just never happened, that's all. I've always been too shy to make the first move."

* * *

Dave gazes at Stephen's turned back for a few seconds then everything slots into place and he gives a soft chuckle.

"Fuck me. A 26-year-old virgin. You must be bunged up worse than that bloody waste pipe of yours I just fixed."

Stephen spins back to face Dave with an anguished wail, long fingers twisting together in agony.

"Aw, just *stop* it, would you? You're making me feel like a freak, here."

Dave regards his discomfort for a moment, then draws up a military plan of action. With a saucy wink, he commandeers the wine bottle off the table and pretends to sneak up on his blushing companion, teasing voice murmuring low at Stephen's flushed ear.

"Well, maybe you are, maybe you aren't. Either way, s'gonna be fun finding out, if you ask me."

Dave shoves the bottle against Stephen's chest making him jump.

"Here. Grab that."

Striding over to the far worktop, Dave tucks the bottle opener into his jeans pocket then extricates the second bottle of wine from the wall cupboard before turning back to Stephen with a grin and a nod toward the stairs leading off the kitchen.

"Boudoir's this way, is it?"

Stephen nods dumbly, his frozen face masking the overwhelming urge to crawl under the sink and hide till the source of his fear gets bored and leaves. In return, Dave gestures towards the stairs again with the bottle, every muscle tensed and ready for action.

"Well, c'mon then. Lead the way. Don't worry, mate. You're in expert hands. I've got a certificate in unblocking things. Think it's high time we got you sorted, don't you?"

Act II
The Cherry-Popping of Patience de Vere

Once upstairs, Dave casts an obviously amused eye around the spotlessly clean surfaces of Stephen's bedroom, not a stray comb, or sock, or deodorant in sight.

"Tidy bugger, ain'tcha?"

Standing rooted to the spot on the doorway's cusp, Stephen feels his shoulders, already painfully tight with anticipation, tensing even further at the perceived criticism.

"I like to keep things *neat*, yes. What's wrong with that?"

With a smile, Dave wanders over to the far side of the bed and deposits his drink and the full bottle of wine on one of the bedside tables. Then, fishing the opener out of his jeans pocket, he starts to uncork the bottle.

"Oh, nothin'. Just observing, that's all. What d'you do for a living, then?"

Knowing he should follow, but completely unable to move his legs, Stephen watches Dave pull the cork from the bottle and place both on the table before testing the bed for springiness with his hand and throwing himself down with a happily contented sigh. For several minutes, Stephen gazes transfixed at the fantasy-sprung-to-life vision of a man stretched feline on his bed. As Dave's eyebrows rise expectantly awaiting Stephen's reply, head propped on one rippling, muscular arm, vest riding up to reveal his washboard stomach, Stephen struggles to remember how to talk, as well as walk. Eventually, he murmurs, "I'm a writer."

"What? Books?"

Snapping out of his lust-filled trance at the silly question, Stephen pulls his gaze away from the tantalising bulge in the crotch of Dave's jeans and snorts derisively, "No, cookery manuals."

"Oh, really?"

For a moment, Stephen contemplates Dave's guilelessly open smile then sighs, guiltily.

"No, sorry, I was pulling your leg. I do write books, yeah. Not the kind of books I'd *like* to write, but books all the same."

Dave pats the bed beside him with a firm hand then raises an eyebrow.

"I'm feeling a bit lonely over here. Y'gonna come and join me, or are y'gonna stand there all night?"

As Stephen takes a deep breath and stumbles forward, his shaking hands make a clattering mess of depositing the half-empty bottle and wineglass on the other bedside table. Instead of joining Dave on the bed, he then retreats to the safe distance of the bedside chair, falling backwards with a *thump*, white knuckles gripping the edges of the seat, wide eyes staring at Dave in open fright.

Across the bedroom, his partner switches body language to relaxed, and vocal tone to pleasant, confusing Stephen further.

"So, then ... what kind of books do you write?"

Stephen sighs, looks to the floor and falls still while wrestling with himself inside. Eventually, when the silence broadcasting his disquiet has grown intolerable, he returns his gaze to Dave, his voice quietly sarcastic.

"Romantic novels. Pot boilers. Bodice rippers. The kind of shit that sells by the bucket load in airports but'll never win you any prizes. I'm not proud of it but it makes me a decent living ... when I haven't got writer's block, that is."

With a chuckle at Stephen's unexpected answer, Dave grabs the wine bottle beside him and refills his glass before taking a slug.

"Give over. What's yer surname, then? My sister's into all that stuff. Maybe I've heard of you."

Stephen gives a rictus grin of discomfort and shakes his head.

"Oh, God, I don't write under my real name. That would be *way* too embarrassing. I write under a *nom de plume*."

In the hush of silence that settles gently on the room in aftermath of this statement, Stephen gradually registers the totally blank look on Dave's face, then tries again.

"You know ... a pseudonym?"

Dave glances up at the ceiling for a moment, seemingly lost in thought, then returns his gaze to Stephen with a cheery smile and a shake of the head.

"Nah, sorry. Still lost. Try English, eh?"

Stephen slumps back in his chair, defeated.

"I write under the pen name of Patience DeVere."

With a resounding hoot that makes Stephen jump, Dave throws himself flat against the bed, his bared stomach heaving with laughter, wine sloshing dangerously close to the rim of his clutched glass.

"Fuck *off*. A-hahahahaha."

Stephen regards him for a moment, trying to recall the remedy for red wine stains on Egyptian linen, forehead furrowing into a fistfight of tension on his brow, then mutters testily, "It's not *that* funny."

This observation is welcomed with open arms by another easy, uncensored hoot of laughter from Dave.

"It bleedin' well *is*. My sister's got a *shelf-load* of your books. The Clarissa Hart novels, they're *yours*, right?"

Shock propels Stephen forward on his chair in double-take, double-quick time, eyes widening in disbelief.

"What? You've *read* them?"

Still chuckling, Dave deposits his miraculously unspilled glass safely onto the bedside table, then props himself back onto one arm to look at Stephen, a dismissive hand wafting in the air between them.

"Nah, nah, 'course not. Not *properly*, that is. Had the odd frisky-fingered-fandango over a few of 'em, mind. Flick straight through to the juicy bits when yer on the loo for a quick trip to Leg Shake Central, y'know? Needs must. Any port in a storm, 'n' all that. How the bleedin' hell do you write all that sex stuff when you've never even *had* it, then?"

Stephen blushes at the vivid mental image of Dave wanking over his carefully honed words and transfers his gaze to his once more fidgeting hands, before muttering tightly, "It's called *imagination*. Maybe you've heard of it?"

Dave's intermittent giggling grows in crescendo to an open belly laugh as another thought strikes him.

"Fuckin' hell. Just wait till I tell dear old Sis I shagged Patience DeVere and she was a *bloke*. Her peepers are gonna pop out of her bleedin' bonce."

Anger steadily rising again in his chest at being made fun of, Stephen glares at Dave, his voice cut caustic with vitriol.

"Well, for starters, you haven't shagged me *yet* and, frankly, your chances of ever doing so are rapidly disappearing up the friggin' Swannee, if you don't stop laughing in the next five minutes."

Noting the edge in Stephen's voice, Dave attempts to headlock his mirth under control and fails miserably, gasping for air.

"Aw, mate ... I'm sorry, I really am ... but you're gonna have to give me the full five minutes ... this is bleedin' hilarious, this is."

Slumping back onto the bed, rubbing his stomach muscles, Dave struggles to breathe.

"Patience DeVere ... a bloke ... a *gay* bloke ... a 26-year-old *virgin*, gay bloke ..."

Snapping, Stephen leaps to his feet.

"Right, that's enough. I think you'd better leave."

Unexpectedly, Dave reaches across the bed with lightning speed to grab Stephen's hand, pulling him off balance and sprawling down onto the bed beside him with a high-pitched, startled yelp.

"Aw ... and I think you'd better keep yer wig on and sit back down. C'mere, you."

Stephen freezes at the warmth of Dave's strong arms clasping around him, gathering him close, too close. The musky scent of Dave's skin in his nostrils stops the breath in his throat as a firmly-muscled thigh presses down on his groin, pinning him to the bed making his cock ache with want as it twitches hungrily in response. Shutting his eyes tightly, Stephen desperately tries not to voice the onslaught of expletives assaulting his brain like a jackhammer as pure panic sets in. Then, Dave's lips are pressing gently at each eyelid, his words soft and warm at Stephen's ear.

"Mate. *Breathe.*"

With a gasp, Stephen exhales, as commanded, and opens his eyes to Dave's concerned face frowning down at him.

"I'm sorry, ok? I didn't mean to poke fun at yer. It just wasn't what I was expecting, that's all. You've gotta admit, it's an unusual job for a bloke to be doing. When I clocked yer expensive kitchen and heard you tapping away at that keyboard, I had you pegged as one of them Internet geeks or something, y'know?"

Warily, Stephen searches Dave's eyes for signs of duplicity and finding none whatsoever, feels his body begin to relax a little in Dave's arms. The wonderful feeling of being held by someone *at long last* beginning to melt the edges of his fear. Eventually, he mutters, "You're the first person I've told about Patience, apart from my agent. *Ever.* So don't go blabbing it about, for fuck's sake. Please?"

With a smile, Dave rubs a gentle fingertip at Stephen's lower lip.

"My lips are sealed, mate. Speaking of which, that's a lovely pout you've got on you there, you know that? First thing I clocked when you opened the door, after yer big, brown eyes."

Dave leans down and murmurs softly at Stephen's ear, "Makes me want to do very, *very* rude things to you."

Shivering at the teasing tickle of Dave's breath on his neck, Stephen gazes wide-eyed at his smiling face as Dave pulls back. Eventually, he gains the confidence to whisper, "Oh, yeah?"

Dave's grin widens, playful, work-rough fingertips tracing spiralling circles across Stephen's cheek and down his neck.

"*Fuck*, yeah."

Dave's grin is so open and infectious, Stephen finds himself smiling in return, the unfamiliar feeling of being desired intoxicating his senses, sending tiny shivers of arousal through his body, switching tensed to electrified, bold.

"Such as?"

With a chuckle, Dave leans down and gives Stephen a smacking kiss on the lips then releases him so he can kneel up on the bed, a playful hand tugging teasingly on the belt loops of Stephen's jeans.

"Well, first off, I think we'd better get you out of these strides, don't you?"

Stephen immediately freezes, a desperate hand flying up to clutch at Dave's wrist.

"Oh, fuck ... hang on a second. Do I have to take them off?"

Dave stares down at Stephen, incredulous.

"What are you on about? *'Course* you have to take 'em off. I know you haven't done this before, but it's bleedin' obvious yer not gonna get yer end away with them *on*, isn't it?"

Stephen hides his face in his hands and groans, "Aw ... *shit* ... it's just, I wasn't expecting this to happen today ... I'm not ... *prepared*."

With a sigh and a fond shake of the head, Dave seemingly decides enough is enough and takes total control. All guns blazing.

"Look, mate. I know you're nervous. We're all nervous first time, believe me. Just relax. Lie back and think of England and let me handle this, ok? I know what I'm doing. You're in safe hands. Promise."

Dave deftly snaps open the button of Stephen's jeans and tugs down the zip, pulling denim from hip until, confronted and confounded by the unexpected, he asks the obvious question.

"Fuck *me*. What the bleedin' hell are you wearing?"

Posture frozen, face hidden, Stephen's reply is moaned in agony, mangle-muffled through still-clutched hands.

"Support tights."

Dave's lower lip drops open in shock, eyes widening in disbelief.

"What? As in *Doris* support tights? Those things birds start wearing instead of sexy undies the *minute* you've gone out with them for more than two weeks and they think they've crossed the finish line? What the *fuck* are you wearing them for? Are you some kind of tranny?"

Stephen's hands fly from his flushed face to land with a *thwack* on the bed, his vehement reply addressed firmly to the light fitting in the ceiling, rather than Dave.

"Yes. I mean *no*. I mean ... *fuck*, this is so embarrassing ... Look. I've got a pot belly, and I hate it, and I can't seem to get rid of it no matter how much I diet. Wearing these flattens it enough to get into skinny jeans, *alright?*"

Voice rising in register and volume, Stephen shifts up onto his elbows to glare at Dave's stunned face.

"Now, you know all my secrets. Just shut the door behind you on the way out, go have a good, long laugh with all your mates down the pub, and leave me alone, *ok?*"

Dave's expression immediately softens, his reply a gentle, placatory murmur.

"Now, why would I wanna do that, eh?"

Cheeks burning, Stephen's dark eyes continue to blaze with the fire of anger fanned by shame as he fails to register Dave's conciliatory response.

"Because, *clearly*, I'm a freak and a saddo who's going to stay a virgin all his life."

Stephen expects the silent, puzzled eye-lock that follows his statement, but is ill-prepared for Dave eventually breaking the deadlock with an easy chuckle.

"Well, I hate to disappoint you, and you may well be right on the first two points, but you don't stand a hope in hell on the third one, mate. That cherry of yours is getting well and truly popped tonight, one way or the other. I'm having *way* too much fun, here. You're priceless, you are. I've never met anyone like yer. Yer a one-off. Now. Where d'you keep yer scissors?"

Stephen's shame and anger are rabbit-punched by puzzlement.

"Kitchen. Cutlery drawer. Why?"

Leaping from the bed, Dave grabs Stephen's wineglass and tops it up from the bottle before placing it firmly on Stephen's chest.

"Here. Have another good wallop of the old Canty-Whotsit to calm yer nerves. And fer Christ's sake, keep breathing, ok? Back in a tick."

Once alone, Stephen stares blankly at the ceiling for a moment in confusion, listening to Dave's footsteps on the stairs and the calamitous clatter of every drawer and cupboard in his kitchen being opened and shut, then sitting up, he drains the entire glass of wine in one. Gasping with shock as the unusually high volume of alcohol hits his stomach, pinning him back onto the bed in a comedy clampdown of relaxation like an all-in wrestler, Stephen starts to giggle.

Hysterically.

His voice emerging a good octave higher than normal.

"Fucking hell. Why isn't he leaving? He should be leaving by now. Could I have done any more to put him off? He must be nuts."

Almost immediately, a new and terrifying thought creeps up and strangles the giggles in Stephen's throat.

"Oh, fuck. That's *it*. He *is* nuts. He must be, to still be here, right? All that stuff about biscuits could have been the ramblings of a mentalist. Maybe that's the speech he gives all his victims before he goes in for the kill. Luring them into his cheeky-chappie, what-the-fuck? world before he pounces. Christ almighty ... oh, shit, shit, *shit*. Why the *fuck* didn't I insist on seeing his ID card?"

Stephen freezes at the sound of Dave's predatory footsteps thumping purposefully back up the stairs, his fatally cheery whistling making the hairs on the back of Stephen's neck stand on end, ready to be cut down in their prime. As Dave comes sauntering back through the door, snipping the air with the scissors like he's brandishing the castanets of death, Stephen gasps,

"What in God's name are you intending to do with those?"

Dave the Mentalist gives a cheeky wink before clambering back onto the bed.

"I'm gonna cut you out of those stupid tights, that's what."

In desperation, Stephen frantically shuffles up the bedding away from Dave the Biscuit Tin Killer — Dave the Sexy Scissor Slasher — as far as he can get, before his back bumps against the headboard, trapping him defenceless.

"Aw, *fuck* ... please tell me you're not a psycho."

Dave stares at Stephen in a look of astounded bemusement for a second before the penny apparently drops along with his shoulders. Eventually, he sighs, his voice patient but firm.

"Steve, mate, I'm *not* a psycho. Can I just point out to yer that *you're* the one lying there in women's undies calling yerself Patience while I'm stood here waving a pair of *nail scissors* at yer, not a bleedin' *chainsaw.*"

Having pondered the sound reasoning of this, Stephen reluctantly switches his inner alarm rating back from red to amber, then shoots Dave a pleading look.

"Look, there's no need for that. I can just pull them off."

Prowling up the bed toward Stephen with a leering grin, Dave takes a firm hold of Stephen's jeans and tugs them off in one, then runs an appreciative eye down Stephen's long, black nylon-clad legs, before murmuring,

"Yeah, but it'll be much more fun this way. Trust me."

Dave runs the edge of the scissors teasingly down Stephen's thigh and calf, laddering the tights into a barcode of shivering, exposed, white flesh as he goes.

"Nice set of pins, you've got on you there. The dancer I shagged in that West End theatre didn't have legs as good as yours, y'know that?"

Eyes widening at the unexpected compliment and the bizarre situation now unfolding, Stephen watches nervously as Dave pulls the nylon clear of the toes on one foot and starts to cut upwards.

"If your hand slips ..."

Snip.

"It won't."

Snip, snip.

"You should know that I'm a bleeder."

Snip, snip, snip.

"You're a funny bleeder, right enough. No arguments on that front."

Snip. Snip. Snip, snip, snip.

"You're getting very fucking *close*, there."

Snip.

"I am, aren't I?"

Snip, snip.

"Oh, Jesus, I can't look."

"Hold tight, Knicker-Twister. One last snip and we're home. Think about it. There's nothing in it for me if I massacre yer crown jewels, is there?"

Snip.

"There. Free at last. One poor squished and, I have ta say, very *kissable* belly and ... hello? One poor squashed but still remarkably hard dick in need of some urgent resuscitation."

The last thing Stephen registers before his eyes slam shut like safety curtains, is his cock disappearing into Dave's mouth, sending his own heart beating, cartoon-like, straight out of his chest. Stephen writhes back into the bed as the warm drag of Dave's tongue and lips burns a laser-path to the pleasure centres in his groin and brain. And it occurs to Stephen that if he could say anything now, apart from, "Fuuuuuuuuuckk," it would be, "Thank you." But neither would stand a chance of being heard above the full-scale "Hallelujah Chorus" now raising the rafters on the Albert Hall inside his head. Instead, Stephen tries to focus on staying conscious and out of cardiac arrest as the suction from Dave's mouth intensifies, one hand slipping under the curve of Stephen's arching back to pull him closer. Tentatively, Stephen opens one eye to the overwhelming sight of Dave moving up and down on him, then he slams it shut again. The image of Dave's glossy, black hair teasing tendril traces across his naked thighs combining with a snapshot of muscular shoulders rising and falling like the waves of pleasure racing through Stephen's body. *Bang.* Burnt in his brain forever.

"Oh, my ... *God* ..."

Then, suddenly, with no warning, the warmth is gone and Stephen shivers, opening his eyes to a cheerily grinning Dave.

"There, now. That's got the old circulation going again, ain't it? Brought a right old rosy blush to yer cheeks, too. You liked that, huh?"

Stephen shakes his head, bewildered.

"You're stopping. Why, *for the love of God*, are you stopping?"

"Easy, Tiger. We've got the whole night ahead of us."

With a quick kiss to Stephen's belly, Dave leaps from the bed again and comes to stand beside him at the head of the bed.

"Ok, stage two: Arms up."

As Stephen raises his weakened arms in surrender, Dave pulls the T-shirt over his head, casting it to the floor before turning back to Stephen with a smile.

"Now, this is the point where you take *my* jeans off."

Trembling at his own nakedness, Stephen sits up and automatically starts to fumble with the button on Dave's jeans, vaguely aware that the communication lines between his reeling mind and his fiddling fingers are well and truly down, and in need of a carrier pigeon. Pronto.

"It's no use. I can't get the button. My hands are shaking too much."

Dave ruffles Stephen's T-shirt tousled hair affectionately and reaches for the empty wineglass on the bedside table, his voice calm and measured.

"Keep trying, you'll get there, mate. Rome wasn't built in a day, as they say. I'll just help myself to another drink, while you improve yer undressing technique. We've all gotta learn some day."

* * *

Having poured himself another glassful, Dave takes a heroic slug then contemplates, in silent amusement, the cat's cradle of confusion Stephen's fingers are steadily weaving themselves into at his waist.

"Fucksake. Why do they make these things so bloody bastard *difficult* to undo?"

As Stephen continues to pull frantically at his waistband, tugging his hips forward, Dave bites down on his lip to silence the chuckle trapped in his throat, hell-bent on escape.

"If I break a sodding nail ..."

Dave buries his face again in his wineglass to hide his smile, then manages to pull himself together.

"So, you'll have a broken nail. So what? Yer such a panic-merchant. Just think of the sense of achievement you'll have at the end of it all, yeah? Not to mention the sense of relief we'll *both* have at the end of it."

"*Yes!* Got the bastard."

The hell-bent chuckle finally finds safe release in response to Stephen's triumphantly grinning upturned face.

"Well done, Patience. Though why you picked that name, I'll never know. Never seen someone get in such a pickle over undoing a simple button."

Stephen's smile of triumph fades instantly and he drops his head, muttering, "Can't help it. I've always been all fingers and thumbs when I'm nervous."

For a moment, Dave regards him silently, noting the arms winding around bare chest for comfort, then he sighs and lifts Stephen's chin, bending down to kiss him gently on the lips.

"You're such a *sensitive* bugger, aren'tcha? Fair do's. I can get a right old stutter going, when the chips are down. One of the reasons I started hanging out with Trevor at school, apart from his God-given ability to drop his trousers at every opportunity, is he didn't make fun of my stammer. Luckily, it got better as I got older. That, and I learned how to thump people. That wiped the laughter off their smug bastard faces."

Locking Stephen's gaze, Dave waits until the smile softening his own lips is returned, then he straightens up, peeling off his vest and tossing it aside before gesturing with both hands at his jeans.

"Well, what're you waiting for? Don't be shy. You know I'm not gonna bite. I think I've proved that much. Now yer in, pull 'em down, then."

Gaining confidence from Dave's encouragement and dragging his gaze from the smooth, hairless plane of his tanned chest, Stephen does as bid, then falls into a silent meditational contemplation of the firm, eye-level bulge in Dave's Calvin Klein's. Eventually, the soft tapping of fingertips on his shoulder pulls him out from his trance.

"And the rest."

Stephen throws Dave a nervous look.

Dave catches it and returns a wink.

Stephen gulps.

Winding his trembling fingers into Dave's waistband, he takes a deep breath and pulls the underwear to the floor, starting backwards as Dave's freed erection jumps to instant attention, nearly smacking him on the nose.

* * *

From some distant universe that he used to belong to, some faraway place where he is not staring directly at another man's naked cock, comes a soft chuckle.

"Like what you see?"

Stephen's head nods of its own volition and switches voice-control to autopilot.

"Yes. Very much. Thank you."

"Want to see what it feels like in yer mouth?"

"Yes, please."

"Well, go on then. Get stuck in."

Clasping Dave's cock in his trembling hands, Stephen shuts his eyes and tries to remember how he used to do this in his dreams, and in his novels. Finding all access to memory banks denied, he decides to go with instinct, mouth parting more in hope than expectation.

Meanwhile, far above Stephen's head, the clouds part, and The God of the Distant Universe speaks.

"Mmmm. I knew those soft lips of yours were gonna feel good."

Stephen feels gentle fingers winding deep into his hair encouraging him to explore further with his quivering tongue, savouring the smoothness of the skin, new-formed synapses in his brain committing the taste-feel complexity to memory. Then, hungry for more, he pulls Dave deeper into his mouth and opens his eyes, wanting to see the reaction. Gazing up, he's rewarded with a beatific smile and languidly lust-lidded eyes, Dave's words mumbled as soft as the fingertips upon his cheek.

"Now move back and forward a bit. Tease me with yer tongue. That's it."

The moan of arousal that is Dave's next response sets every light in Stephen's head to green. Clutching a hand to the taut behind he was so entranced by earlier, Stephen pulls Dave closer and takes him deeper, lost in the intensity of his movements and Dave's responding gasps until a frantic hand grips tightly at his head.

"Christ, mind the teeth there, mate. I bleed, too, you know."

Stephen's eyes dart nervously to Dave's, but once again find only good humour and twinkling arousal, encouraging him to continue.

"That's better. Aw, man. That is good. That is really fucking *good*. Don't stop with that."

Soothed by Dave's moaned, mumbled mantra, Stephen settles into a rhythm. And it drifts through Stephen's mind that he could quite happily do this all day, if it wasn't for the slow ache of cramp creeping into his jaw — a feature of oral sex never mentioned in novels, for some odd reason.

Stephen is pulled out of his reverie by Dave's panting voice overhead.

"Steve, mate ... I'm gonna come soon. You've got three choices, here, ok? Spit, swallow or duck. Spit means you let me come in your mouth and spit it out. Swallow's obvious. And duck means you get the hell away from the danger area when I say, 'now.' Got that?"

Mind reeling at Dave's list of instructions, Stephen tries to get in urgent contact with the part of his brain that used to make decisions but finds the office shut and no one home. Before he can think of an alternative plan, an equally urgent voice cuts across his panic.

"*Now!*"

In pure fight or flight response, Stephen pulls clear just in time to watch Dave come, bucking and trembling in his grip, head thrown back, strong hands clutching onto Stephen's shoulders for support. Stephen watches mesmerised, his other hand once again at Dave's behind to stop him falling backwards, lost in the wonder of seeing another human being lose himself in ecstasy. When the shuddering in Dave's body, held in his trembling hands, finally stops, Stephen whispers, "Sorry, I couldn't decide on the first two options, so I thought the third was the safest bet."

Dave's head slowly drifts forward again, his flushed and grinning face making Stephen's heart perform a little hop-skip of delight.

"For yer first time, that was definitely the safest bet."

Dave leans down and kisses Stephen slowly and lazily, warm lips smudging gratitude across cheek and forehead.

"Congratulations, my friend. You just gave yer first blowjob. And very good it was, too. A right old knee-trembler."

Dave straightens up and smiles affectionately at Stephen's upturned beaming face.

"Look at you, all pleased with yerself. Woops, gave you a right old pearl necklace there. Sorry 'bout that. Better clean you up a bit, eh? Here, lie back."

Dave waits for Stephen to shuffle backwards on the bed, then straddles him, his teasing tongue snaking an upward path along Stephen's belly, heading for his chest, then mouth. Stephen squirms and giggles softly at the tickling, then his eyes widen in disbelief as Dave sets about his neck and shoulders.

"You're gonna *lick* it off me?"

"Mmm hmm."

"What does it taste like?"

"Snog me and you'll find out."

Pushing his tongue between Dave's lips, it drifts through Stephen's mind that although he's written hundreds of sex scenes, the one key thing he never realised until this moment, is that sex is all about reaching inside another person, breaking down the exterior walls of propriety to make contact with what is hidden. The gift — another human being allowing you to do that. The penalty — once in, you carry their gifted vulnerability, their imprint, forever. The challenge — to open up in return and be kind to them, if what they show you isn't what you want.

That, and getting your rocks off, obviously.

Stephen drinks in the taste of Dave, the feel of Dave and wonders if he is up to receiving the gift, paying the penalty and meeting the challenge as much as he's up for getting his rocks off.

"Like it?"

Stephen opens his eyes to Dave's smiling face gazing down at him and makes his decision.

"I could get used to it, I think."

"Oh, I'll bet you could, Sunshine."

This time, as Dave kisses him, Stephen feels himself fully relax into the embrace, simply enjoying the slow-burn graze of stubble against his lips and the caressing movement of Dave's tongue in his mouth. Instinctively, he runs his hands down Dave's smooth shoulder blades to massage the curve in the small of his back, making Dave rumble-groan into his mouth.

"Aw, fuck, yeah. *That's* the spot. How did y'know my back was hurting?"

Stephen smiles shyly and murmurs, "I didn't. I just did it without thinking."

Dave grins.

"*Now*, yer getting it. Don't get me wrong, I'm all for thinking, but this is one area of life where it gets in the way. Shagging's not about thinking; it's about *doing*. That's the way I see it, anyway. Ok, now lift yer legs and hold 'em like that with yer arms."

"Why?"

"I'm gonna show you something else you could get used to."

Stephen's eyes widen as Dave reaches over the end of the bed to extract the tin of cleanser from his jeans pocket.

"What do you need that for?"

Dave gives a cheeky wink and unscrews the tin.

"Yer not the only one who wasn't ready for this happening today. This, my friend, is called jazz improv."

Having watched Dave's preparation in stunned silence, pondering in puzzlement what possible link could exist between John Coltrane and proprietary cleanser, Stephen then gasps in shock as Dave's cold, gel-slicked finger begins to boldly go where no man has gone before.

"Oh, Dave, I don't know about this. That feels funny."

Dave's gently probing finger takes one small step for man, one giant leap for mankind.

"Just relax, mate. There are three stages to this. First it feels a bit funny, as you say ..."

"Ow!"

"Then it feels a bit painful, sorry, but that's when you've really got to relax, ok? Don't tense, don't fight me, yeah?"

"Shit!"

Dave's fearless exploration of inner space hits a setback — a crushing vacuum makes him wince in agony. *In space, no one can hear you scream.*

"*Relax*, I said. If you clench any tighter, I'm gonna lose a fuckin' finger,

here. *Jesus.* Have another slug of that Vino Collapso and just chill a bit, ok? I'm not pushing any further until you do. That's a promise, alright?"

This time, Stephen's hands are shaking so badly, he deposits most of the wine onto the bed with no thought of Egyptian linen, before throwing the remainder down his throat.

"Sorry. I'm just so nervous. What if I shit myself?"

"You won't. At least, you'd fuckin' better *not.* That's a bit specialist, even for me."

Dave starts to stroke Stephen's cock gently with his other hand in time to his words, his voice soothing.

"Just *calm* yourself, ok? Breathe *deeply.* Stop *panicking.*"

Eyes fixed firmly on the ceiling, Stephen wonders when he acquired *two* light fittings and how come they seem to be moving of their own accord?

"Ok. Ok. I can do this. I can *do* this ... God, I'm drunk. I normally only have a couple of glasses a night."

Stephen watches, hypnotised, as the light fitting(s) waltz merrily like funfair rides, his body relaxing again under the alcohol's onslaught, then he starts to giggle uncontrollably.

"Mind you, normally, I'm not lying on my bed with a plumber's fingers up my arse."

Explosive, warm laughter pulls Stephen's gaze away from the ceiling to stare instead at the dancing light in Dave's eyes.

"That's the beauty of this life, my friend. Always expect the unexpected. When I jumped out of bed this morning, full of the joys of spring, I didn't know I'd end the day shagging a bloke in tights who calls himself Patience DeVere, did I now?"

While Stephen is busy chuckling, Dave takes advantage of his relaxation to restart the engines and press forward again.

"Fucking hell, Dave, life's weird, when you stop to think about it, isn't it?"

"Yup, Steve, my friend. Weird as fuck. That's why most buggers never stop to think about it. They're too bloody scared of losing it completely, if they do. But, we're not thinking here, remember? We're *doing.* Now, the next stage of this is where it starts to feel really fucking good."

Retro boosters on.

"Just about ... *here*."

Space station docked.

"Bloody *Nora!*"

"Exactly. *Now*, yer glad you relaxed, aren't yer?"

The stars in Stephen's field of vision explode in time to the movement of Dave's fingers deep inside him and Dave's caressing hand around his cock.

"Fuck, yeah. *Please* don't stop doing that."

"Oh, I've no intention of stopping, mate. Don't you worry."

As Stephen feels the warmth and suction of Dave's mouth closing in on him again, he shuts his eyes and gives himself over to the waves of pleasure sweeping through his body, vaguely aware that someone, somewhere, is making one hell of a racket and it can't possibly be Dave. And it occurs to Stephen that while he may have waited 26 long years for this moment, it was well worth the wait, as his body bucks of it's own volition back onto Dave's fingers and deeper into Dave's mouth until the disembodied voice screams, *"NOW!"* in a manner that Stephen knows will have the neighbours gossiping for weeks.

"Fucking hell, Dave. That was ..."

As Stephen realises there are no words for what just happened, he feels Dave's warm lips mumbling softly at his belly.

"A damn sight better than a lonely wank in front of 'Torchwood,' love. Think you might be venturing out the house a bit more from now on?"

Stephen winds grateful fingers deep into Dave's hair and makes a life-changing resolution.

"I'm never watching telly again."

Dave's grinning face emerges from its place of rest on Stephen's tummy.

"Wise decision, mate. Now, for future reference, it's even better if you can get a cock up there, only I didn't want to push my luck. You're gonna have to learn to relax a damn sight more until yer ready for that. I'm only just getting me circulation back. Where's yer bathroom?"

"First door on the left."

"Back in a tick."

Stephen mutely watches Dave depart, making a mental note that if he ever gets a second chance, those back dimples are getting a damn good licking, then lets out a long sigh of release and tries to get in touch with the rest of his brain. Feeling suddenly freezing, he stands up on shaking legs and gets properly into the bed, wrapping the wine-soaked duvet around him for warmth, the sound of the bathroom taps distant-running echoing the cold wash of comedown in his body. At last, his long-lost brain reopens communication with a startling thought.

I did it. I finally fucking did it. I'm not a virgin anymore. Yes!

Stephen bundles the edge of the duvet into his mouth to muffle his joyous laughter, then feels a tug on the fabric and opens his eyes to a grinning Dave climbing into the bed beside him. Dave reaches over to switch off the bedside light then shuffles down closer to Stephen, warm, strong arms once again gathering him into an embrace.

"C'mere, Laughing Boy. Give us a cuddle. I'm shattered, been up since six this morning. You don't mind if I crash here tonight, do yer?"

"'Course not."

Stephen snuggles against Dave's chest then remembers his manners.

"Dave?"

"Hmmm?"

"Thank you."

Dave chuckles and plants a kiss in Stephen's hair.

"No problem, mate. Enjoyed it. Like I said, yer a one-off. Sorry it took me 26 years to come and fix yer blockage but, better late than never, eh? Sodding London traffic. Night night."

As Dave shuts his eyes and starts to drift into the arms of Morpheus, Stephen stares into the black-hole darkness of Dave's chest, wide awake. Reactivated brain suddenly awash with questions, swiftly followed by doubts, and finally chased by fears. Listening to Dave's breathing gradually, slowly deepen, his warm chest rising and falling at Stephen's cheek, Stephen realises it's now or never. When he eventually plucks up the courage to speak, his voice is tentative and whispered at the confessional grail of Dave's skin — Dave's responses, increasingly mumbled and sleepy as a child's bedtime prayer.

"Dave?"

"Hmmm?"

"Do you do this a lot on jobs?"

"Nah. Just occasionally, like I said."

"When you do, do you ever see them again?"

"Not usually, no."

"But ... the odd time, you do?"

"The odd time, yeah."

"How does that work, then?"

"Oh, I'll leave one of me tools under their sink or something. Gives me the excuse to pop back."

Dave gives Stephen's shoulder a squeeze and smudges a weary kiss at his head, his softly whispered words drowning in the encroaching tidal wave of inescapable unconsciousness.

"Look, I'm knackered mate, and I've got an early start again tomorrow. I know yer all excited but try to get some sleep, eh?"

"Night, Dave."

Stephen waits for a response, then realising Dave has finally fallen asleep, tries to focus on the security of physical warmth that surrounds him instead of the chill of mental insecurity freeze-forming in his head. His tentative lips secretly searching out the softness of Dave's slumbering skin to hopefully leave a kissed trace of himself on Dave forever.

* * *

"Oooowwww ... my *brain* hurts ... Jesus..."

Stephen opens his eyes to a coruscating supernova of light, then shuts them tight again with a wince of pain.

"*Fuuuuuck ...*"

Gradually, the slow retina-burnout fades to leave the deeply depressing image of an empty bed phosphene-emblazoned on the inside of tight-shut eyelids. With a weary sigh, Stephen hauls himself upright and out of bed.

"What the fuck did you expect, you idiot? Did you really think he'd hang around? You've been writing romantic novels so long, your brain's turned to mush. This is reality, my friend."

Stephen stumbles into last night's jeans and traipses dejectedly down to the kitchen, clinging to the banister for support. The overwhelming need for painkillers driving his feet forward, eyes still half-shut in protest at the painful light of day. Staggering into the kitchen, Stephen makes his way towards the far cupboard then comes to a howling halt as the open door of the sink unit connects with tender shin.

"Ow! Jesus! *Shit!*"

Collapsing rag-dolled to the floor, Stephen rubs at his bruised ankle, the pain in his leg connecting with the pain in his head and heart, making him want to cry — if only his dehydrated body could produce enough water for tears.

"Right. That's it. Today's cancelled. Painkillers. Bacon butty. Bed. In that order. Clarissa's gonna have to stay in that bloody garden of hers for another 24 hours with her tits heaving. Today, I am Captain Duvet not Patience-friggin'-deVere. Fuck it. Fuck everyone. Fuck everyth—"

This time, Stephen's solitary rant dies strangled in his throat before the front door can intervene. Because, before him, very obviously placed to be noticed at the front of the sink cupboard, lies Dave's ratchet.

Resting his chin on tucked up knees, Stephen regards the forgotten tool in silence for several long minutes, the tick of the kitchen clock *tocking* in time to the thump of his heart. Eventually, he whispers, "Don't get your hopes up."

Rising to his feet, Stephen's voice rises with him.

"Do. Not. Get. Your. Hopes. Up. You're a fucking idiot, if you think he left that there on purpose. We had a shitload to drink last night. He probably just forgot it."

Stumbling to the kettle, Stephen flicks the switch on and opens the wall cupboard to fetch a mug, then gasps in surprise.

At the front of the cupboard, gate-crashing the regimented crockery, sits an uninvited pair of pliers. In a daze, Stephen pulls out a mug and shuts the cupboard door.

"We were *really* shit-faced. Monged. Bladdered. Don't be fucking stupid. Don't read anything into this."

As the kettle whistles to a boil, Stephen flicks on the radio, smiling at a familiar tune, then reaches into the cutlery drawer for a teaspoon and pulls out a spanner instead.

Heart now racing, Stephen methodically flings open every drawer and cupboard in his kitchen. In each one, Dave has left one of the tools of his trade.

Suddenly, miraculously, Stephen doesn't feel hungover any more. Instead he starts to grin. The grin buckles into a chuckle. The chuckle gives way to a laugh. The laugh steps aside for a mini-breakdown.

"He likes me. He fucking *likes* me. Me. Me. *Me*. The tranny. The saddo. The *freak*."

Hooting with happy laughter, Stephen tosses the lid off the coffee jar, grinning as it clatters its way across the marbled worktop, then he messily plonks two heaped spoonfuls into his mug along with three scattered sugars. Hop-skipping across to the fridge, he reaches inside for the milk, finds the tin of proprietary cleanser instead and cracks up.

"Mr. Support Tights. Ms. Patience DeVere. God's Gift to Plumbing likes *ME*. A-hahahahaha …"

Breakfast finally made, Stephen places everything on a tray and flicks off the radio. Shimmying into the lounge, still whistling the beloved tune as he goes, he fires up his computer and munches happily at his toast while everything launches. Then, clicking his way into his writing folder, he freezes, crestfallen. The sudden, sickening sight of "To Hell for Love — Clarissa Hart novel No.13" draining the smile from his lips and the colour from his cheeks.

Stephen sits for a moment in silence, slowly sipping his coffee, eyes fixed on the treacherous little yellow folder, so much struggle and despair wrapped up in one innocuous icon. Then he makes a decision. Placing his coffee cup down, Stephen clasps the mouse in his hand and right-clicks to bring up the menu.

Stephen sighs deeply.

Then he breathes again.

Then he hits "delete."

As the folder defiantly holds its ground on the desktop, Stephen's computer takes it upon itself to ask the obvious question, since, clearly, the person operating the mouse has lost control of his sanity.

Are you sure you want to delete "To Hell for Love – Clarissa Hart novel No.13" and move all its contents to the recycle bin?

Staring at the onscreen words, Stephen murmurs softly to himself, "*Am* I sure?"

Taking another long slug of coffee, he grips the mouse with a shaking hand, the fear of finality freezing his fingers immobile on the aluminium surface. Wrestling with what to do inside, his eyes drift to the weekly shopping list on his desk, his gaze alerted by something odd and out of place. At the bottom of the familiar list of neatly typed items such as lettuce, wine and tights, Dave has added in a handwritten looping, rounded scrawl, *Fondant Fancies, beer and condoms.*

Stephen grins and grips the mouse tighter.

"Yes. I'm fucking sure. Sorry, Clarissa. It's over, love. Been nice knowing you. But we've grown apart."

Stephen clicks "*yes*" and smiles as the folder disappears from the screen.

Then, another thought strikes Stephen, and he starts to giggle. Courage and conviction mounting, he right-clicks the recycle bin to bring up its own menu.

"Truth is, love. I've been having it off with my plumber and he's 10 times the man than you'll ever be. See ya."

Stephen clicks "*empty the recycle bin*" and lets out a long, relieved sigh. Draining his coffee, he then opens a new Word document and starts to type, fingernails gleefully tap-dancing all over the metallic keyboard with the lightness he feels in both head and body. Fast fingers flying to convey the unfettered joy he feels in both heart and soul.

The Biscuit Tin Philosopher
A novel by Stephen Patterson
First Draft: 13/7/10
Chapter 1

This world is weird as fuck when you stop to think about it. And the weirdest thing is, hardly any fucker does. Stop to think, I mean. For instance, I met a man once who based his entire philosophy of life around biscuits, dividing all humanity into Digestives, Bourbons and chunky Kit Kats. Now, I know what you're thinking: You're thinking he was insane, right? Wrong. He was the sanest man I ever met, and meeting him changed my life ...

About the Author

Cameron Vale is one of the pen names used by a London-based polymath and autodidact who has thoroughly researched all the best ways to fall asleep on a keyboard. Cameron would like it known that although she may well have some Stephen Patterson in her, she has never ripped a bodice in her life.